This igloo book belongs to:

_____

Published in 2013
by Igloo Books Ltd
Cottage Farm
Sywell
NN6 0BJ
www.igloobooks.com

SHE001 0713
10 9 8 7 6 5 4 3 2 1
ISBN: 978-1-78197-070-6

Printed and manufactured in China

# Stories
## for little
# Princesses

igloobooks

# Contents

# Princess Fiona's Fashion Show

Princess Fiona looked around the busy dressing room happily. It was full of princesses, all stitching, chattering, giggling and trying on dresses. Tonight was the night of Fiona's first ever fashion show and all of her princess friends had come to take part in it. "Do you think my dress looks okay?" asked Princess Ella, looking at her lovely, shiny, purple gown. "The front is a bit plain." "It just needs something extra. How about this purple flower?" said Fiona, choosing one from the table filled with pretty dress decorations. "I'll stitch it on for you."

After she'd sewn on Ella's flower, Princess Fiona helped all of her other friends finish their outfits. She ran from dress to dress, adding sequins here and buttons there until everyone looked fantastic.

Princess Fiona was so happy that everything was ready, until suddenly, she remembered her own dress. Fiona hadn't decorated it at all. It was completely plain! She hurried to the decorations table and reached for some fabric paint. Fiona squeezed the tube, but instead of a neat line of paint, a huge splodge came bursting out. "Oh, no!" she cried, looking at the fabric paint splattered all over her dress.

## Princess Fiona's Fashion Show

As fast as she could, Princess Fiona snatched up the dress.
She was going to run to the sink and try to wash the paint off,
but as she moved away from the table, her dress caught on a basket
of cotton reels. Everyone gasped as the sleeve ripped right off.
"Oh, no," cried Fiona. "I've completely ruined my dress! I worked so
hard to organize the fashion show and now I can't be in it!"

Princess Fiona started to sob. "Don't cry, Fiona," said Princess Ella, kindly. "Everything will be ok. Let's get you a drink of lemonade and have a rest before the show starts."

"Thanks, Ella," said Princess Fiona, with a sniffle and a small smile, as Ella led her away. Behind them, the other princesses were whispering to one another. They'd suddenly had a fantastic idea.

# Princess Fiona's Fashion Show

"Why don't you have a look in the dressing room?" asked Princess Dani, when Fiona returned. "There might be a spare dress for you in there."
"I don't think there is," sighed Princess Fiona, "but I'll check anyway."
Fiona walked into the dressing room and couldn't believe what she saw. Her dress had been repaired with sparkling sequins and pretty bows. The other princesses must have fixed it while she was away. "Oh, thank you so much!" cried Fiona.

All the kings and queens had come to watch the fashion show.
The princesses all wished each other luck, as the audience sat admiring
the beautiful stage decorations Fiona had made. They were so excited.
Princess Fiona started the music, then signaled for the princesses to
walk out on stage. They each strutted down the runway and then
posed at the end, just like real models.

The audience clapped and cheered and soon,
it was Fiona's turn to walk out in her beautiful dress.
"Hooray!" cried the audience, when she appeared on the stage.
"Well done, Princess Fiona!" Princess Ella handed Fiona a big bunch
of flowers and Fiona giggled. She was so proud that the show had gone
fantastically, but even more proud to have the best friends ever.

# Princess Daisy and the Dragon

Princess Daisy was just starting her new book when Prince George stumbled into her reading room, dressed in his pretend suit of armor. He knocked over everything in his path as he clanged and clanked around. "Oh, George!" Daisy cried. "Look what you've done!"

"I am Sir George the Brave," said George, waving his sword wildly, knocking Daisy's mug of hot chocolate over onto a stack of her books. "No!" cried Daisy, picking the mug up. Her books were soaked. "Please be more careful, George!"

"I can't be too careful," said George. "I have to seek out every dragon, wherever they are, then fight them!"

Daisy put her hands on her hips and frowned. She was fed up of her things getting broken because of George's pretend dragon fights. "Why don't you just go outside and find a real dragon to fight with, George?" she huffed.

Princess Daisy and the Dragon

"Okay, I will," said Prince George, knocking over another vase as he stomped outside. Princess Daisy sighed and started clearing up the mess that George had left behind.

When the room was back to normal, Daisy flopped down into her armchair and picked her book back up. "Finally, I can carry on reading," thought Daisy. She had just got to a really good part of her book, when she heard a very loud ROAR from outside.

# Princess Daisy and the Dragon

Princess Daisy rushed outside, just as Prince George raced past the doorway. "HELP ME, DAISY!" he yelled. "I found a real dragon and now he's after me!" Sure enough, a tall, red dragon was racing across the palace grounds behind George. He had little, purple wings and yellow scales down his back. STOMP, STOMP, STOMP, went his big feet. The dragon was breathing smoke and running after George like he wanted to gobble him up.

Princess Daisy gasped. She'd told George to go looking for real dragons and now he was in danger. It was all her fault! She had to help him, fast. Bravely, Daisy stepped between Prince George and the dragon and put her hands firmly on her hips. "STOP!" she cried, trying to pull a mean, scary face. "Bad dragon! Leave George alone. Go away!" Daisy closed her eyes tight and waited for the dragon to grab her with his pointy claws.

# Princess Daisy and the Dragon

To Daisy's surprise, the dragon didn't grab her. Instead, there was a screeching, slobbering sound and then Princess Daisy felt hot breath on her cheeks. Slowly, she opened her eyes. The dragon stood right in front of her face, with a huge tear rolling down his cheek. "I don't want to eat anyone," said the dragon, in a wobbly voice. "I was just chasing after him to say I want a friend to play with. I'm so lonely."

Princess Daisy couldn't believe it. The dragon just wanted to be George's friend! "I'd love to play with you, Mr Dragon," laughed Prince George, "and maybe my sister Daisy will play with us, too." From that day, George and his dragon played together all the time. They stomped and trampled all around the palace grounds, scaring the birds, the rabbits and even the royal gardener.

## Princess Daisy and the Dragon

Best of all, they loved to play knights and dragons. They had so much fun searching for scary monsters and hidden treasure together and at long last, Princess Daisy could read as many books as she wanted without being disturbed. The only thing was, George's dragon was so much fun that sometimes she just had to go outside and play with him, too.

# Princess Sophie's Shoes

Princess Sophie was very excited. She had been invited to her friend Princess Jessica's birthday party and was planning her outfit.

"I'll definitely wear my best pink party shoes," thought Sophie, happily. She found her shoes and tried to put one on, but even though Sophie squeezed and squashed her foot, the shoe just wouldn't fit.

Just then, Sophie's friends Princess Katie and Princess Amber arrived. "What's the matter, Sophie?" asked Amber, seeing Sophie's glum face. "Ooo, I love your shoes!" Sadly, Sophie told Amber that they didn't fit.

"Oh, no," said Katie. "We brought these to show you. They're our shoes for Jessica's party."

Katie and Amber's shoes were beautiful. "My mother has got loads of lovely sparkly shoes with pretty heels," sighed Sophie. "I wish I could wear them, but she says I'm too young."

# Princess Sophie's Shoes

Princess Sophie tried on all of her other shoes, but none of them looked right with her lovely party dress. Her sneakers were too tatty, her boots were far too clunky and all of her pairs of flat shoes were really very boring. So, when her mother went out for the afternoon, Sophie tiptoed along the corridor and sneaked into the queen's grand dressing room. She knew she would be able to find plenty of fancy pairs of party shoes in there.

# Princess Sophie's Shoes

The queen's dressing room was filled with beautiful high-heeled shoes. Sophie saw a perfect purple pair, with a bow on the front. "They would look amazing with my party dress," she gasped. Sophie carefully tried them on and immediately wobbled about. Then, she tried taking a step, wobbled more and fell over. Determined to walk in the shoes, Sophie picked herself up, tried one more time and fell over again with a BUMP.

Princess Sophie was very sad. When the queen came home, Sophie was sat in the throne room in tears. The princess told the queen that she didn't have any shoes to wear to Jessica's party. "I even went in your dressing room while you were gone," said Sophie. "All my friends have bought lovely, new shoes and your purple high-heels match my dress perfectly. I tried them on, but I kept falling over."

## Princess Sophie's Shoes

The queen told Sophie not to cry and gave her a big cuddle. "Now you see why you can't wear high-heels yet. They're very hard to walk in," said the queen, kindly. "Come on, I've got lots of other lovely things you can dress up in." With a sigh, Princess Sophie followed the queen back to her dressing room. She tried on the queen's hats, handbags, crowns and scarves, but she still felt sad. She would have no pretty shoes to wear to Princess Jessica's party the next day.

# Stories for Little Princesses

The next afternoon, Princess Sophie got ready for the party. She put on her dress and picked out a lovely handbag to carry. "Oh, don't you look wonderful!" cried the queen, when she saw Sophie in her outfit. "I've got a special surprise to show you before you go to the party. Don't forget!" As soon as Princess Sophie was ready to leave, the queen took her into the throne room and told her to close her eyes.

## Princess Sophie's Shoes

When Sophie opened her eyes, she saw the palace handyman in front of her, holding a pair of sparkly, purple shoes. "We made these for you! They match mine exactly," said the queen, "only without the heels." "They're beautiful!" cried Sophie. "Thank you both so much!" The shoes fit perfectly and Sophie couldn't wait to show her friends. In fact, Sophie was so delighted, her smile almost matched the sparkle on her shoes.

# Princess Mia and the Spooky Ghost

Princess Mia was very excited. All of her princess friends were coming round for a very special slumber party. They were going to have a midnight feast with cupcakes, sandwiches, all sorts of candy and plenty of pink lemonade. Best of all, they were going to dance around to cool music and have lots of pillow fights.

Mia happily helped the royal cook prepare some treats and then rushed up to her room to make sure everything was neat and tidy, ready for the princesses. As Mia watched the royal butler and maid carrying lots of things around, she picked up Kitty, her beautiful, fluffy kitten and gave her a big cuddle. "We're going to have so much fun tonight, Kitty," said Mia, with a huge smile.

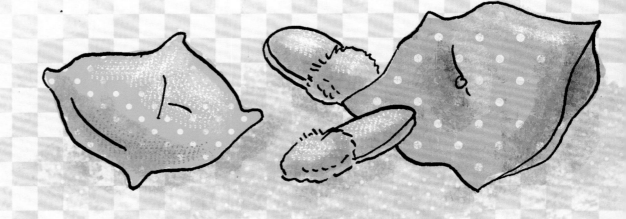

When the other princesses arrived, they were all as excited as Princess Mia. They changed into their pajamas straight away and spread their sleeping bags and big, squashy pillows out over Mia's bedroom floor. Then, the princess friends played games until late at night. They had a big pillow fight and sang along to the pop songs they liked best. It was brilliant fun.

# Princess Mia and the Spooky Ghost

"How can we stay awake til midnight to have a feast?" asked Mia.
"We could tell each other spooky stories," suggested Princess Chloe.
First, Princess Paula told a vampire story. Then, Princess Lizzie
scared everyone with stories about monsters and witches.
Finally, Mia told them about the ghost who clattered around the palace
at midnight, searching for princesses to haunt. "No more stories!"
cried Princess Chloe. "I'm getting scared!"

The princesses soon decided it was time go to sleep. Everything was very quiet and then, suddenly... CLATTER! BANG! CRASH!

"What was that?" cried Princess Paula.

"I think it's Mia's clattery ghost," whispered Chloe, as the clock in the hallway spookily struck midnight.

"Well," said Mia, standing up. "There's only one way to find out." The princesses followed Mia as she bravely tiptoed downstairs, heading straight towards the noise.

CLATTER! BASH! Everyone jumped as they reached the downstairs floor of the palace. "The noises are coming from the kitchen," said Princess Mia in a whisper. "Come on, everyone. Let's give the ghost a big surprise!" Everyone held their breath as Mia bravely pushed open the door. Suddenly, she burst out laughing. Kitty was on the kitchen worktop, happily climbing across all the pots and pans she'd knocked over.

Everyone laughed and Princess Mia gave Kitty a huge cuddle.

"What's all the banging?" asked the maid, rushing into the room.

"I wondered if we were being haunted by a noisy ghost!"

"No ghosts, just one naughty, noisy kitten," said Mia, giggling.

"Well, while you're all down in the kitchen, you might as well have an extra-special midnight feast," said the maid.

# Princess Mia and the Spooky Ghost

The maid and the butler whizzed up some yummy hot chocolate,
with big swirls of whipped cream and marshmallows to go on top.
Mia put out all the treats that she and the royal cook had made earlier
and everyone enjoyed the tasty food. Even Kitty tried a slice of cake!
The princesses all agreed, Mia's slumber party had been the spookiest
and the most fun slumber party ever.

# The Magic Necklace

Princess Luna loved to dance. She practiced her steps, twists and leaps all over the palace and she always had so much fun going to dance class with her princess friends. One day, her teacher, Miss Tiptoe, announced they'd be putting on a special show. Luna was so excited. "Luna, why don't you try dancing at the front this time?" said Miss Tiptoe. Luna couldn't believe it. She'd always danced at the back before, behind her friends.

Miss Tiptoe taught the princesses the routine that they would be performing in the show and Luna concentrated hard. She did a twirl, a leap and two sideways high kicks. Then, Luna realised no one else was doing the same moves as her! Was she supposed to start with a twirl or a jump? She couldn't remember the routine and without her friends in front of her, Luna had no one to copy.

Princess Luna practiced and practiced at home, but she couldn't remember the order the moves went in. Everyone was going to see her get it wrong in the show. Luna felt so upset. "What's the matter?" asked her grandad, worriedly. Luna told him all about her routine. "I know just the thing!" said Grandad, giving Luna a long necklace with a beautiful star pendant. "This is a magic memory necklace. If you wear it, you'll remember all the moves."

# The Magic Necklace

Princess Luna decided to give the magic necklace a try. She put it on and practiced again. Suddenly, she found herself remembering more and more of the whole dance routine. It really was magic!

Luna wore her necklace to her next dance class and confidently performed every twist, jump and twirl in just the right order.

"Well done, Luna!" cried Miss Tiptoe. "That's much better than before. I think you're going to be fantastic in the show!"

# Stories for Little Princesses

Princess Luna practiced her steps every day until, finally, it was the day of the big show. Princess Luna couldn't wait to get on stage. With her magic necklace helping her get everything right, she knew the show would be fantastic. When Luna was dressed in her costume, she unzipped her bag to get out her necklace, but it wasn't there. "Oh, no!" she cried. "I can't have lost it!" Desperately, Luna tipped her bag upside down, but the sparkly star pendant was nowhere to be seen.

# The Magic Necklace

Grandad went backstage to wish Luna luck and found her in tears.

"What's the matter now, Luna?" he asked.

"I can't find my magic necklace anywhere!" Luna sobbed. "If I'm not wearing it, I'll get everything wrong."

Grandad chuckled and gave Luna a hug. "No you won't, silly," he said. "Your necklace has helped you learn the routine off by heart. Remember how you felt when you were wearing it and you'll be fine!"

Princess Luna wiped her tears away and tried to feel brave.
As she stepped out onto the stage, Luna thought about what her
Grandad had told her and suddenly, her nerves disappeared.
The music started and Luna performed each dance step perfectly,
with a big smile on her face. She had so much fun and by the end,
the audience were on their feet clapping and cheering.

# The Magic Necklace

"Well done, you clever girl!" cried Grandad, once the show was over.

"I didn't need my necklace after all," said Luna, proudly.

Grandad smiled and said, "I've got a secret to tell you. The necklace isn't really magic. I just said that to give you confidence." Luna giggled happily. She felt more confident than ever and would never be worried about her dance moves again.

# Princess Bella and the Ball

Princess Bella was very upset. "Why do I have to go to the stupid Spring Ball?" she asked her mother, with her hands on her hips. "Bella, the Spring Ball isn't stupid," said the queen, looking at their invitation happily. "You like dancing. There'll be lovely music and lots of really tasty food. All your friends will be there, too. I'm sure you'll have great fun."

Bella frowned. She did like dancing, as well as climbing trees, playing football and rollerblading, but she wouldn't have great fun at the ball. That was because she knew she would have to wear a silly, frilly dress. Bella just wasn't a dress-wearing sort of princess. She had to walk carefully and sit just right when she wore one. You couldn't climb trees wearing a big, lacy dress.

# Princess Bella and the Ball

Hundreds of different dresses were delivered to the palace for Princess Bella. "There must be something you like out of all these," said the queen. "If it's too long or doesn't fit right, the royal seamstress can change it." With a big sigh, Princess Bella tried on stripy dresses, puffy dresses and dresses with lots of frilly layers. She hated them all. "I just want to wear my dungarees," she sighed.

# Princess Bella and the Ball

The day before the ball, the queen announced she had a special surprise for Bella. "I had this made especially for you!" she cried, holding up a purple dress, the shade that Bella liked best. When Bella tried the dress on, it didn't look too bad. In fact, Bella was so comfortable in it, that she ran outside to play and accidentally splattered the dress with mud. "Oh, no!" cried Bella, as she reached the top of the tree house.

The next day, the maid announced that the stains on Princess Bella's dress wouldn't wash out. "Well, I'm not going to the ball then," said Bella to the maid, with a frown. As she stomped away, Princess Bella spotted the queen looking sad. Suddenly, Bella felt very sorry for how she had behaved. The queen had tried so hard to find a dress for her to wear. She would be so disappointed if they didn't go to the ball.

Suddenly, Princess Bella had an idea. She rummaged through
her wardrobe, pulling out all kinds of clothes. Then, she searched
through her arts and crafts things, to find sequins and beads.
Bella managed to put together a whole heap of glittery decorations.
Then, she found a basket full of glitter pens and fabric paints.
She would have to work quickly to be ready in time for the ball.

Everyone was already at the Spring Ball when Bella and her parents arrived. Lots of guests turned to look at Bella's unusual outfit as they walked into the ballroom. She was wearing her dotty leggings, a purple tutu and an orange t-shirt that was decorated with fabric paint, sparkly sequins and glitter patterns. Bella glimmered and shimmered as she twirled onto the ballroom dance floor.

# Princess Bella and the Ball

"Bella isn't wearing a dress," whispered the other princesses and princes, "but her outfit is really cool!" The king and queen watched happily as Bella's princess friends admired her customized clothes. Bella danced all evening with her friends and had a great time, just like the queen had said she would. Even though she wasn't wearing a dress, Princess Bella had turned out to be the belle of the ball!

# Princess Penny and the Surprise Party

It was the king's birthday and Princess Penny was planning a surprise party for her dad. She wanted there to be lots of lovely food for everyone to eat. She tiptoed down to the kitchen before the royal cook was awake and started making jelly sandwiches. Penny had made quite a few, when the royal cook opened the kitchen door. "Oh, Princess Penny!" she cried. "You've made such a mess! Let me make those sandwiches for you!" "No, thanks," said the princess. "I want to do it all by myself."

Penny carried on making sandwiches, but after a while, she had to admit, they looked very messy. The bread had got all sticky with big blobs of jelly. "Oh, never mind," said Penny. "I'll make some decorations next and finish the food later."

# Princess Penny and the Surprise Party

Princess Penny decided to make some pretty bunting. She cut out triangles of fabric, but somehow they seemed to stick to everything but the string. "What are you doing?" asked the royal seamstress. When Penny told her, the seamstress smiled and said, "I could sew the bunting for you if you'd like."

"No, thanks," said Penny. "I want to do it all by myself."

## Princess Penny and the Surprise Party

After a while, Princess Penny gave up on her bunting. All she had made was a big, sticky, tangle of string. "I'll blow up some balloons instead," she said to herself, with a sigh. Penny thought that there was nothing that could go wrong with some plain, old balloons, but they were much more difficult to blow up than they looked. They kept popping loudly in Princess Penny's face, with bits of balloon flying everywhere!

When Princess Penny had popped every balloon in the packet, she burst into tears. All she'd wanted to do was give her dad the best birthday surprise ever, but she couldn't do anything right! The royal maid rushed into Penny's bedroom when she heard the princess crying. "Don't worry," said the maid kindly, when Penny told her what was wrong. "You tried your hardest."

# Princess Penny and the Surprise Party

Princess Penny didn't feel any better, though. The king's party
was still ruined, whether she tried hard or not.
"Why don't you make the king a birthday card before he gets up?"
suggested the maid. Penny smiled. Her dad loved home-made cards
and she could always give him a big birthday cuddle, too. She dried
her tears and quickly set to work making him a pretty card with
a picture of a cake on it.

Princess Penny finished the card and ran to find the king. She spotted him walking outside into the palace garden. Just as Penny caught up with the king, he cried, "Wow! This is wonderful!"

The garden had been decorated with lots of balloons and beautiful bunting. There was a delicious spread of party food on the table, too. Princess Penny couldn't believe her eyes! Where had everything come from?

"I spoke to the royal cook and seamstress," the maid whispered in Penny's ear, as the king looked around excitedly. "We fixed everything for you, as a surprise, because you were so thoughtful and tried to do it all by yourself!" Penny felt so happy as she watched everyone tucking into the party food. She gave the king the birthday card she had made and he was delighted. It really had turned out to be the perfect birthday surprise after all!

# Princess Tina's Buried Treasure

Princess Tina was fed up and so was Princess Chrissie. They wanted to play games with the king and queen, but their parents were too busy talking about money, which was really boring. "The roof over the kitchen needs mending," sighed the king, peering at a list of repairs. "It's going to be very expensive. Can't we just leave it?" "No!" cried the queen. "Poor Cook gets soaked from head to toe every time it rains!"

"Can you play hide-and-seek with us yet?" asked Princess Tina. "Not yet," said the queen. "Why don't you play together for a while?" "Maybe you'll find the royal treasure that's been lost for years," sighed the king. "That would be helpful!" The princesses didn't hear him say anything, though, because they were already running off across the grounds to play.

# Princess Tina's Buried Treasure

63

Chrissie and Tina had been running about for a while, when
their puppy, Pickles, started woofing and digging at the ground
by a tree. "Pickles has found something!" cried Princess Tina.
"It's a treasure chest," gasped Princess Chrissie, as Pickles dug
more mud out of the way. The sisters heaved the chest out of the
ground and pulled the lid open. It was filled with glittering
necklaces, rings, bangles, tiaras and all sorts of treasure.

# Princess Tina's Buried Treasure

The princesses couldn't believe their eyes. "Pickles, you are so clever," squealed Tina, hugging him tight. "This jewelry is really beautiful. Let's try everything on."

The sisters carried the chest to their bedroom. They giggled as they put on their best dressing-up clothes and piled on the jewels. Then they danced and jangled all around their bedroom.

"Let's show Mom and Dad our costumes," said Tina. "Maybe that will cheer them up." The princesses crept into the room where their parents were chatting. "Surprise!" shouted the sisters, as they jumped out in front of their parents. The king and queen both gasped and stared with open mouths when they saw the princesses' outfits.

# Princess Tina's Buried Treasure

"You've found the missing royal treasure!" cried the king, hugging Tina excitedly. "We won't ever have to worry about money again!" "We can fix the leaking roof after all," said the queen, scooping Princess Chrissie up into her arms, "and the rest of the palace, too." The princesses laughed happily and told the king and queen that it was clever Pickles who had uncovered the lost treasure, not them.

The jewels the princesses had found were worth a fortune.
"While we're repairing the palace, we could build you your very own
dressing-up room, if you like," the king told them, "and you could
design it." Princess Tina and Princess Chrissie were so happy.
They gave their dressing-up room enormous mirrors, cupboards
and wardrobes filled with funny costumes and beautiful dresses.
They chose a carpet to go along the runway and cool stage lights.

# Princess Tina's Buried Treasure

Even Pickles had lots of dressing-up outfits to choose from. Tina and Chrissie made sure that he would always join them on the runway when they put on a fashion show, no matter how grumpy he looked in his funny costume. The king and queen always had plenty of time to watch the sisters now that they didn't have to worry about the palace. For the princesses, that was the best part of finding the treasure after all.

# Princess Rachel and the Royal Wedding

Princess Rachel was very excited. Finally, the big day had come. It was the wedding of the year and Rachel had been looking forward to it so much. The beautiful Princess Angelina was marrying handsome Prince Rupert and Rachel had been invited. "I wonder what Princess Angelina's wedding dress will be like," said Rachel excitedly, as the queen helped her put on a new outfit. She could hardly keep still as the queen curled her hair and tied a ribbon into a pretty bow on top.

Princess Rachel loved weddings. She thought everything about them was magical, from the bride's big, white dress to the confetti that fluttered through the sky. Best of all, Rachel liked the beautiful flowers that the bride and bridesmaid would carry. She hoped that one day, she would be a bridesmaid, carrying a bouquet and following a happy bride down the aisle.

When Princess Rachel and her parents arrived at the wedding, they saw lots of important guests in their fanciest outfits. Everyone eagerly looked to see if Princess Angelina was on her way. Finally, the royal horse-drawn carriage arrived and everyone gasped at how beautiful the bride looked. Princess Angelina had an elegant, white dress with lots of sequins and she was carrying the prettiest bouquet.

# Princess Rachel and the Royal Wedding

The horse that pulled the royal carriage thought the flowers looked lovely, too. As Princess Angelina walked past him, he took a great big bite out of her bouquet. "Chomp, chomp, chomp," went the horse, looking very happy as the flowers disappeared into his mouth.

"Oh, no!" cried Angelina, holding just the stalks of her flowers.

"What am I going to do? A bride can't get married without a bouquet!"

# Stories for Little Princesses

Princess Rachel had an idea. She hurried into the little meadow next to the church and picked bluebells, lavender and lots of big white daisies, as fast as she could. Then, Rachel pulled the ribbon out of her hair and tied the flowers together with a pretty bow. Finally, she gathered even more flowers and quickly twisted them together, to make garlands for the bride and bridesmaids to wear in their hair.

# Princess Rachel and the Royal Wedding

Princess Rachel hurried back to the bride, who was almost in tears.
"Princess Angelina?" said Rachel. "I found you some flowers. You could use them for your wedding, if you like."
"Oh, thank you so much!" cried Angelina, beaming happily at Rachel.
"They're beautiful." Rachel giggled and blushed, as she helped Princess Angelina put the flower garlands into the bridesmaids' hair.

"I've made a spare garland," said Princess Rachel, as she fixed the last bridesmaid's hair, "just in case one gets lost."

Princess Angelina smiled. "Well then I know just how to thank you," she said. "Would you like to be an extra bridesmaid, Rachel?"

Rachel couldn't believe it. She was finally going to be a bridesmaid, at the most wonderful wedding of the year. "Yes, please!" she cried.

# Princess Rachel and the Royal Wedding

The other bridesmaids' dresses were just like Rachel's. She didn't even look too out of place next to them! Quickly, Princess Angelina helped Rachel fix the last garland in her hair. Then, the happy bride walked down the aisle, clutching her beautiful bouquet of wild flowers. She was followed by three happy bridesmaids, but the one with the biggest smile of all was Princess Rachel.

# The Baking Competition

Princess Cassie loved to bake. She would spend whole days trying to make tasty cupcakes, sticky iced buns, jam tarts and crunchy flapjacks, but somehow, nothing ever turned out quite right. Cassie could never keep things in the oven for the right amount of time, or whisk up cream until it was thick, or get her sponges to rise up nice and high.

One day, Cassie's best friend Princess Flora told her about a princesses' baking competition. "Entering a baking competition would be great," she said, "but what if my cake is a disaster?"
"Why don't we bake our cakes together?" Flora suggested, with a smile.
"Then we can help each other." Cassie thought it was a brilliant idea and the princesses started mixing up two fruity sponges, one with oranges and one with strawberries.

# The Baking Competition

Princess Cassie was so excited as she waited for her strawberry cake to cook. When it finally came out of the oven, Cassie couldn't believe her eyes. Flora's cake looked perfect, but hers was an ugly, lumpy mess. All over the cake, strawberries were sticking up out of the mixture, burnt and crispy. "Never mind," said Flora. "We'll cut off the horrible bits and make frosting to spread over our cakes. They'll look beautiful."

# The Baking Competition

Cassie and Flora each whipped up a bowl of frosting. Flora spread hers onto her sponge in a neat, swirly pattern. Cassie tried her hardest, but somehow splattered the frosting out of the piping bag and all over the kitchen. There wasn't enough left to cover her cake. "I can't take this big, splodgy mess to the competition!" cried Cassie.

"Never mind, Cassie. You can make another one," said Princess Flora. "Well, this time I'll make two cakes," said Princess Cassie, "just in case one goes wrong." Cassie quickly mixed up a blueberry cake and a chocolate-chip one. The mixtures smelled very yummy, but when they came out of the oven, one cake had bubbled up like a cloud and the other had a huge split down the middle. "I'm so useless at cooking," cried Cassie, bursting into tears.

# The Baking Competition

"Don't worry!" Flora cried. "I've got an idea! Make more blue, orange and pink frosting. Double what we had before." Cassie didn't see how that would help, but she did as Flora said. Her frosting still went everywhere, but this time there was plenty left for the cake.

"Now, sandwich all three sponges together," said Flora, as Cassie started to stack the cakes, "and they'll make one big, super-splodgy, fruity-chocolatey, spongey tower cake!"

Princess Cassie and Princess Flora excitedly took their cakes to
the princesses' baking competition. Cassie couldn't help but gasp
as they walked past table after table of beautiful cakes, in every
different shape and size. "They all look so yummy," said Cassie,
with a sigh. "My cake doesn't stand a chance."
"Well, we'll just have to wait and see," said Flora, giving her
friend's shoulder a big squeeze.

Soon, the judges had tasted all of the cakes and chosen the winners.
Cassie was delighted when Flora's orange cake won first prize.
"We've also decided to give out a special rosette for the Most
Creative Cake of All," the judge said. "It goes to Princess Cassie's
very unusual but tasty cake tower." Cassie couldn't believe it.
She gave Flora a huge hug and together they tucked into their
prize-winning cakes, the best bakers at the competition after all.

# Princess Sara's Big Surprise

Princess Sara loved dogs more than anything. All her life she'd longed to have a puppy of her very own to look after, but the queen said the palace wasn't the right place for one. "A puppy might break all of my lovely ornaments," the queen would say, anxiously, "or it might bark and frighten important visitors away."

One day, Sara spotted a beautiful, white dog with brown patches, bouncing all around the palace garden. She hurried outside and as soon as the dog saw her, he woofed excitedly and ran over, dropping a stick at her feet. "Where have you come from?" said Sara, laughing as the dog tried to lick her. She threw the stick and the dog ran to fetch it, his tail wagging. Then, Sara spotted a ball in the bushes and held it up high in her hand. She giggled as the dog bounced as high as he could, trying to reach it.

# Princess Sara's Big Surprise

Princess Sara named the dog Patches and they played together all
through the afternoon. He learned his name very quickly and came
running whenever Sara called him. As the sun started to go down,
Patches ran through some bushes. He didn't come back when Princess
Sara called his name. She felt so disappointed. "Maybe Patches will
come back tomorrow," she thought.

# Princess Sara's Big Surprise

Every day, Princess Sara looked out for Patches, but he didn't come back to her garden. One day, Sara searched the palace grounds, just in case Patches was hiding somewhere. She was just about to give up looking, when suddenly, Sara heard a woof coming from the stables. Excitedly, she opened the door. It was Patches, but he didn't come running over to say hello. He just lay on the hay, looking very ill and sad.

Princess Sara raced back to the palace and found the queen in her sitting room. "You've got to come to the stables quickly!" cried Sara. "There's a dog there and he looks really ill. I think he needs help!" "Oh, dear," said the queen, rushing to her feet. She put on her boots, wobbling around and fussing with the laces for ages. Sara pulled the queen along, not wanting to leave Patches alone for another minute.

# Princess Sara's Big Surprise

They raced across to the stables, but when Princess Sara opened the door, she got a huge surprise. Next to Patches, there were four cute, little puppies. "He was a she all along," said Princess Sara, crouching down to stroke a puppy. "Patches, you clever girl!" "No wonder she didn't look well, if she was having puppies," said the queen. "I think she belongs to Prince Edmund, who lives in the palace across the river. I'll call him straight away."

Prince Edmund hurried over to Sara's palace. "How wonderful!" he cried, when he saw the puppies. "Well done, Patch!" So Patches was called Patch after all. Princess Sara was happy that she'd guessed her name almost exactly right. "Thank you for looking after Patch," said Prince Edmund to Sara. "I'll have to think of a way to repay you."

# Princess Sara's Big Surprise

He thought for a moment, then asked, "Would you like to keep one of Patch's puppies, maybe?" Sara gasped and looked at the queen, who giggled and nodded, as the puppies climbed all over her. "I'd love to!" cried Princess Sara. Edmund handed her an adorable puppy and Sara hugged him happily. Finally, she had a dog all of her own.

# The Dressing-Up Day

Princess Lucy and Princess Francesca were sisters. They had so many fun games that they would play together around the palace, but best of all, they loved to play dressing-up. The two princesses liked to run around in the funniest, silliest costumes they could find.

In a wardrobe in their bedroom, the princesses had built themselves a fantastic collection of fancy-dress clothes. They had stacks of hats in all different shapes and sizes, feathery scarves, stripy tights and all sorts of silly shoes.

One day, Princess Lucy was pulling things out of the cupboard, when she had a good idea. "Why don't we try and make Mom and Dad laugh by dressing up in silly costumes?" she asked her sister.

"That's a great idea," replied Princess Francesca, as she bounced on her bed in a giant suit jacket. "What shall we dress up as first?"

# The Dressing-Up Day

When they were all dressed up, the princesses ran outside into the palace gardens in their costumes. They giggled as they hid behind a fountain, waiting for their parents. "I'm a magical mermaid!" yelled Princess Francesca, jumping out as the king and queen strolled past. "Arrr, I'm a scary pirate!" cried Princess Lucy, waving a toy sword. The king and queen shrieked. "You made us jump!" cried the queen.

# The Dressing-Up Day

The princesses liked surprising the king and queen. At lunchtime, the sisters carried tea and sandwiches over to their table. "Lunch is served, Your Highnesses," giggled Lucy, dressed as a maid.

"This soup is the finest, most delicious soup in all of the kingdom," said Francesca, pretending to be a snooty chef.

"Of course it is, Madam Chef," said the king, "or is that you, Princess Francesca? I just can't tell!"

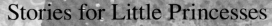

Finally, the twins planned the biggest dressing-up surprise of all.
They snuck quietly into the king and queen's sitting room and each
hid behind a big, blue throne. "Shhh!" said Princess Francesca, when
Princess Lucy started to giggle. "We'll ruin the surprise if we don't
keep really quiet." Just then, the king and queen walked in and
turned on the sitting room lights.

# The Dressing-Up Day

"SURPRISE!" cried Lucy and Francesca, jumping out and onto
the king and queen's thrones. "We dressed up as you!"
The king and queen laughed. The royal chef and the maid thought
that the princesses looked very funny, too. "You look just like us,"
said the king, "and now if we ever need a day off, we know that we
can just get you two to pretend to be us instead!"

# Princess Patsy's Stormy Birthday

Princess Patsy looked around her garden excitedly. Today was the day of her birthday party and all her friends were coming. Everything was ready for them to arrive. There was a huge bouncy castle, balloons everywhere and, best of all, a giant, delicious birthday cake.

As Patsy walked next to the bouncy castle, she suddenly heard someone muttering. It was Princess Lauren from next-door. "I wish I didn't have to go to this party," she heard Lauren say. Patsy frowned. Lauren had just moved in next-door and she was so grumpy. She never even spoke to Patsy over the fence and now she was complaining about coming to the party. Princess Patsy stood next to where Lauren was playing on her swing and glared at her as meanly as she could.

Suddenly, the wind blew hard and it started pouring with rain.
Princess Patsy raced inside. She gazed miserably out of the window
as her birthday cake got soaked and the bouncy castle was deflated.
Thunder crashed and lightning flashed as the rain poured down
from gigantic storm clouds. "I'm sorry, Patsy," said the queen.
"All your friends have phoned to say that they can't come to the party
because of the terrible storm."

# Princess Patsy's Stormy Birthday

Princess Patsy was so upset. Her lovely party was ruined.
Just then, the doorbell rang. "Someone made it after all! Hurray!"
cried Patsy, running to the door. She flung the front door open,
only to see grumpy Princess Lauren and her mother standing in
the doorway. Lauren only had to travel from next-door, so she'd
had no problem getting to the party. Patsy was so disappointed
that she felt like crying.

# Stories for Little Princesses

Princess Patsy and Princess Lauren sat sulkily on the sofa while their moms chatted. Patsy didn't even know why the queen had invited Lauren in the first place. She looked miserably at the uneaten party food and grabbed a strawberry cupcake. "Would you like one?" she said to Lauren, just to be polite. Lauren smiled.

"Thanks, Patsy," she said, quietly. "I love strawberry cupcakes."

"Me too," said Patsy, smiling back.

# Princess Patsy's Stormy Birthday

"I think that pink is the best color," said Princess Lauren.

"Me too," said Princess Patsy. "I got these pink shoes for my birthday."

"Wow!" cried Lauren, admiring them. "They're fantastic."

Patsy's mom smiled, as she saw the two girls talking. "Why don't you two play some fun party games?" she asked. Princess Patsy put some cool pop music on and the two girls danced all around the palace, playing musical statues and hide-and-seek.

"Patsy, the sun's shining again!" called Patsy's mother. The two princesses ran out into the palace garden. It had stopped raining and the sunshine had dried out the bouncy castle. Together, Princess Patsy and Princess Lauren leapt all over the bouncy castle, giggling happily. "Thank you for inviting me to your party," said Lauren. "I would have asked you round to play, but I'm really shy. I didn't think you'd ever want to play with me."

# Princess Patsy's Stormy Birthday

"Don't be silly," said Patsy. "I just thought you didn't like me. I'm sorry I didn't ever invite you over to play either."

Lauren giggled and said, "It's a shame the rain spoiled your party."

"I don't mind," said Patsy, smiling at Lauren. "A party in the sunshine would have been really lovely, but if it hadn't rained we would never have become friends!"

# Princess Pippa's Teddy

Princess Pippa loved her Teddy so much, they went everywhere and did everything together. They would spend sunny days zooming across the palace grounds on Pippa's bike or her skateboard. Sometimes, Teddy would accidentally tumble into a muddy puddle. "Oops," Pippa would say, scooping Teddy out of the mud and cuddling him. "Silly Teddy. You fall off everything!"

One afternoon, Princess Pippa decided to have her lunch in the garden with Teddy. The royal cook brought Pippa a plate of cupcakes with creamy frosting and a jug of delicious pink lemonade, too. "These cupcakes are amazing!" cried Pippa, flinging her arm up in the air and knocking lemonade all over Teddy. "Oops, sorry Teddy," said Pippa, with a giggle.

# Princess Pippa's Teddy

Later, Princess Pippa went to play with Princess Julia and Princess Lisa in the castle next-door. Together they painted pictures and played board games. As Julia and Lisa's toy giraffe and hippo joined in with the fun, Pippa felt bad. Her friends were so gentle with their soft toys, but Pippa didn't look after Teddy anywhere near as carefully. She'd even left him behind at the palace today, instead of bringing him along to play with her friends.

# Princess Pippa's Teddy

When Princess Pippa got home, she looked for Teddy straight away. He wasn't in his usual place on her bed. Pippa searched for Teddy behind her chair and in her toy box, but he was nowhere to be seen. Then, Pippa spotted something pink and fluffy under her bed and pulled it out. It was Teddy! "I must have knocked him underneath my bed without even noticing," thought Pippa, sadly.

Princess Pippa realised just how tatty Teddy had got. His stuffing was popping out and his fur was muddy. "I'm sorry, Teddy," said Pippa, starting to cry. "I haven't looked after you very well at all."

Pippa's sister, Princess Felicity, heard Pippa crying. "I've let Teddy get really tatty," Pippa told her, sobbing. "I'm the meanest princess ever!"

"Don't worry," said Felicity, with a smile. "We'll put it right."

# Princess Pippa's Teddy

Princess Felicity helped Princess Pippa run a foamy bubble bath.
They put Teddy into the hot, soapy water and squeezed all sorts of
shampoos, lotions and fruity shower gels onto his fur. Then, Felicity
scrubbed Teddy with a brush and Pippa swished him around in the water,
until he was squeaky clean and all the dirt and lemonade was gone.
Teddy was so dirty that he turned the bathwater brown and purple!

When Teddy was dry, Princess Felicity ran to fetch her sewing kit and all of her best fabric. Together, the two sisters stitched a patchwork square onto Teddy's side to stop his stuffing coming out. Then, they sewed him a smart new bow tie. "We just need one more thing," said Felicity, rushing off to her bedroom and coming back with a little, golden crown. "It's from my princess doll. It will fit Teddy perfectly!"

# Princess Tessa's Teddy

Felicity giggled, as she put the crown onto Teddy's head. "Just like a prince!" cried Princess Pippa, happily. She gave her lovely, squashy Teddy a big cuddle, then, she put him down and gave Princess Felicity an even bigger hug. "Thank you, Felicity," said Pippa, as her sister looked at her with surprise. "Teddy looks even better than he did when he was new. You're the best big sister in the whole world!"

# The Ballet Bedroom

Princess Kate and Princess Beth were twins who were definitely not identical. Kate loved ballet and singing and everything neat and pretty. Beth liked anything that was really messy, like painting with big, splodgy paintbrushes, or junk-modelling with lots of sticky glue and glitter. The twins shared the same bedroom and while Princess Kate kept her things tidy, Princess Beth didn't care if her things went everywhere. She would leave paints and paintbrushes where she'd finished using them and sometimes even squish glue all over the floor.

"Girls, you really need to be a bit tidier," said the queen, when she saw their bedroom one day. Kate agreed, but she was fed up of clearing away Beth's mess. "Beth, please tidy up your things," said Kate, with her hands on her hips.
"Oh, I'll do it later," Beth said. "I'm too busy now."

The Ballet Bedroom

When Princess Beth refused to tidy up, Princess Kate usually gave up straight away and did it herself. This time, she'd had enough. Beth had to learn to take care of her own things! "Fine," said Kate, smiling and folding her arms, "but I'm busy too, so I'm not tidying anything up either. We'll just have to let the room stay messy until we've both got time to do a bit of cleaning."

# The Ballet Bedroom

Slowly, the twins' bedroom got messier and messier. Clothes, toys and rubbish piled up everywhere. Soon, Princess Beth couldn't even see where she had left her paints. "This is horrible!" she wailed. "Sorry, Beth. I'm off to ballet, then I'm going to a slumber party," replied Kate, as she walked out of the door. "Don't worry, we can just leave the tidying till later!"

# Stories for Little Princesses

"Kate is being so selfish," thought Princess Beth to herself, crossly climbing over all the rubbish. "She's left me to clear this mess up all by myself." Then, Beth suddenly realised how mean she had been. Kate had always tidied her things up for her and she had never even said thank you or offered to help! "I know just how I can make it up to her," thought Beth, with a big smile.

# The Ballet Bedroom

Princess Beth hurried to find the royal handyman, with a long list of all the different things she would need to arrange a special surprise for Princess Kate. "Can you help me?" she asked. "I need paints, brushes, flowers, string, a really big piece of paper..." The handyman looked at the list and smiled. "No problem, Princess Beth," he said. "I can help you with the work, too, if you'd like."

When Princess Kate got back from her slumber party, she walked
upstairs feeling glum. She wasn't looking forward to being in the messy
bedroom again. "Wow," gasped Kate, when she opened the door.
Not only was the room tidy, but there was a beautiful ballerina
painting on the wall beside her bed, plus flowers, pretty cushions
and decorations everywhere. "Surprise!" cried Princess Beth.

# The Ballet Bedroom

"Oh, Beth, this is wonderful! I can't believe you did all this while I was away," said Princess Kate, with a giggle. "Thank you! I couldn't imagine a prettier bedroom. You're a wonderful sister."

"I haven't been very kind to you for a while," said Princess Beth, giving Kate a big hug, "but I've changed now. And I promise our bedroom will never be messy again!"

# Princess Hattie's Hungry Pony

Princess Hattie loved her pony, Stardust. She'd had him since she was little and she rode him whenever she could. Together, they explored the palace grounds, the fields and the woods beyond. There was only one problem. They always had to stop for Stardust to eat! Stardust chewed everything he could find, whether it was flowers, nettles, twigs, or even tasty treats from a stranger's picnic. Hattie was often very embarrassed by how naughty Stardust could be. Even when Stardust was put away in his stables, nothing was safe from being munched on.

One day, Princess Hattie went out to visit Stardust, only to spot him behind the stables, chomping away at the king's beautiful prize-winning sunflowers. By the time Hattie could stop Stardust, the flowers were almost all gone.

"You've got to stop being so naughty or the king will say you have to go," Hattie told Stardust crossly, leading him back to his stable. Then, she had an idea. Princess Hattie brought lots of hay inside the stable to give Stardust plenty to eat. If he had enough to munch on, maybe he wouldn't try and escape again. Even though there was a whole wheelbarrow-full of hay to eat, Stardust munched his way through it in a flash.

# Princess Hattie's Hungry Pony

At least all Stardust's eating gave him lots of energy.
When Princess Hattie rode him in the Royal Show Jumping
Competition, he was the only pony to jump all the fences without
knocking any down. Hattie was delighted. "Well done, Stardust!"
she cried. She showed Stardust the rosette he had won, but Stardust
just tried to eat it, much to the surprise of the competition judges.

The next day, the queen and the royal cook whipped up some delicious frosted cupcakes. Following the tasty smell, Stardust snuck out of his stable and gobbled a cupcake through the open kitchen window.

"Oh, Stardust," huffed the queen. "You're so naughty!"

Princess Hattie was very upset when she came running to see what Stardust had done. "You'll be taken away from me if you don't learn to behave," she said to Stardust, sadly.

# Princess Hattie's Hungry Pony

"Hattie, of course we won't take Stardust away," said the queen.
"Stardust is very cheeky, but he makes everyone laugh, too. We all
love him. We have to keep him!" Princess Hattie was so pleased.
Everyone loved Stardust, despite his naughtiness. She could keep
him forever. Hattie gave Stardust a lovely, shiny apple to munch on
and a big hug. Of course, Stardust just chomped down the apple and
then started to nibble on Hattie's hairband, too!

# Princess Summer's Ice Cream Disaster

As she hurried across the palace grounds, Princess Summer felt so pleased. It was the day of her charity fair and the sun was shining brightly. Summer had organised the fair all by herself, with just a little help from some of her princess friends.

All the other princesses were already at their stalls when Summer got to hers. She was so glad that she had such kind, helpful friends. "What a lovely day!" cried Princess Zara, as she decorated her hook-a-duck stand. "I'm sure lots of people will come to the fair now!" Summer really hoped so. She happily set up her ice cream stall and then helped the royal servants carry out cool-boxes filled with chocolate, strawberry and banana ice cream. As the fair opened, every cloud in the sky disappeared, the sun shone even more brightly and crowds began to flock to the stalls.

It was so hot, Princess Summer's ice cream stall was the busiest of all.
People queued to buy cones topped with sprinkles and once they'd
eaten them, many came back for more. It was non-stop work and soon,
Summer was very hot and tired. She glanced at her friends, who were
chatting together by the palace. They had all sold everything on their
stalls, but none of them had come to help her.

# Princess Summer's Ice Cream Disaster

When her princess friends walked into the palace without even saying where they were going, Summer wanted to cry. Then, she noticed that the parasol over her stall wasn't shading the ice cream properly and it was all starting to melt. Soon, a big puddle of ice cream had formed in front of Summer's stand. "Oh, no!" she cried, as a prince slipped over in the puddle with a huge SQUELCH.

Before long, Summer had completely run out of toppings, ice cream and cones. "I'm sorry," she told a little boy who'd queued for an ice cream for twenty minutes. "I haven't got anything left." He burst into tears. Summer started to cry, too, when she thought of all the extra money she could have made for charity if she'd had someone to help her. The king rushed over to see what was wrong.

# Princess Summer's Ice Cream Disaster

"I've run out of ice cream and none of my friends are here to help me," sobbed Princess Summer.

"Yes, we are!" cried a voice from the palace doors. Summer couldn't believe her eyes. It was Zara and the other princesses, rushing towards her with arms full of ice cream tubs. "The royal servants are bringing a big parasol to give us more shade," said Princess Alice, cheerfully. "Now we can sell much more ice cream and raise lots of money for charity."

Everyone in the queue for ice cream cheered and Princess Summer smiled delightedly. So that's what her friends had been chatting to each other about earlier! Every one of Summer's princess friends helped her serve ice cream. The servants brought lots of exciting, new toppings over, too, like white chocolate chips, rainbow sprinkles, mini marshmallows and strawberry sauce.

When the princesses ran out of cones, they made ice cream sandwiches and sundaes in fancy glasses. They sold hundreds of ice creams and raised so much money for charity. "Do you know what I love even better than ice cream?" Summer asked her friends, as they scooped and served. When they all shook their heads, Summer giggled and answered, "Having the best friends in the world!"

# Princess Rosie and the Talent Competition

Princess Rosie loved to listen to music. She always had the coolest pop songs booming out of the speakers in her bedroom and posters of bands stuck over every wall. Pretending that her hairbrush was a microphone, Rosie loved to sing and practice her dance moves in front of her mirror. She sang beautifully, but very loudly, too. In fact, the servants all wore earplugs whenever they had to go near Rosie's room.

One day, Rosie's teacher made an exciting announcement. "The school is going to hold a talent competition," she said. "Everyone is welcome to take part, whatever their talent is." Rosie was so excited. When she got home that night, she couldn't stop thinking about entering the competition with a band of her very own. "I'll get my friends to be in the band with me," thought Rosie. "I bet we could win a prize if we practiced hard enough."

At school the next day, Princess Rosie asked her friends to form a band.
Princess Jenny played guitar, Princess Caroline played the drums and
Princess Holly played piano better than anyone else she knew. They all
loved the idea of being in Rosie's band! "Can I join, too?" asked
Princess Olivia. "I can't play an instrument, but I could be the lead singer."
Rosie was disappointed. She really wanted to be the lead singer, but she
couldn't leave Olivia out. "Of course you can," she said, with a smile.

# Princess Rosie and the Talent Competition

At every band practice, Princess Rosie stood to one side, playing the tambourine. She would have loved nothing more than to be the lead singer of the band, but Princess Olivia looked like she was having so much fun. Besides, she had a lovely singing voice, too. Soon, the band sounded fantastic. When they practiced for a final time, Rosie handed out cool costumes that she had made for everyone all by herself.

On the evening of the talent competition, the princess friends met up
in the auditorium. Everyone was excited, but then, Princess Olivia
ran over looking very worried. "I've just seen the crowd outside,"
she cried. "It's huge! I can't sing in front of all those people.
I'm just too nervous. I'm so sorry, Rosie. Will you sing instead?"
"Oh, please sing, Rosie," said the other princesses. "You're the only
one who knows all the words!"

# Princess Rosie and the Talent Competition

Princess Rosie agreed. She had to sing, or the band couldn't perform at all! Together, they went out on stage when their name was called and played the song just like they had rehearsed. It sounded fantastic! The audience cheered and clapped loudly and when the song finished, they shouted, "Encore!" and stamped their feet. Rosie couldn't believe it!

There were so many fantastic acts in the talent competition, the princesses had no idea who was going to win. As the judges announced that they had chosen the winners, Princess Rosie and her friends waited anxiously for the result. When the band didn't come third or second, Rosie was really worried. Then, the judges cried, "The first place winner of the talent competition is... Princess Rosie, with her amazing band!"

# Princess Rosie and the Talent Competition

The audience cheered louder than ever before. "We did it!" cried Princess Caroline. Princess Olivia rushed over to Rosie and gave her a huge hug, while the other princesses collected the first-place trophy. "Thank you for singing for me at the last minute," said Olivia. "You have the most fantastic singing voice!" Rosie felt so happy. Winning the contest was brilliant, but she was even more glad to have such lovely friends.

# Princess Maria and the Magic Goggles

Princess Maria wandered around her family's new palace feeling miserable. Moving palace was bad enough, but leaving her friends behind was worse. Now she had no one to play with. Maria wandered glumly up to the attic, the only room in the palace she hadn't explored yet.

"Wow!" cried Maria, as she walked into the attic. It was filled with strange, unusual objects. There was a model ship, a trident, an old oar from a boat and in one corner, a chest with an anchor on the side. Princess Maria opened it and found that it was filled with the prettiest shells. As she looked through them, Maria found a pair of diving goggles, right in the middle of the chest. They fitted her perfectly. "Maybe I could go diving in these," thought Maria, looking out of the window at the lagoon in the palace grounds.

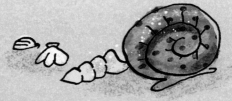

Princess Maria changed into her swimming costume and hurried outside, where the king and queen were already relaxing in the bright sunshine. As she sat down at the edge of the lagoon and dipped her legs in the water, Maria could see pretty, little fish swimming all around her feet. The lagoon was beautiful.

"I wish I had friends here to swim with me," sighed Maria.

# Princess Maria and the Magic Goggles

Maria put on the goggles and dived into the clear, blue water. She swam deep down, spotting lots of stripy fish as she went. Suddenly, Maria saw something completely unbelievable. At the bottom of the lagoon, there was a castle made of shells, with three beautiful mermaids swimming next to it. As Maria watched them in amazement, the mermaids smiled and waved to her.

"Hello!" cried one mermaid. "I see you're wearing the magic diving goggles from the palace. Only people who wear them can see us and enter our world. My name is Lavender."

"I'm Ruby. Come and visit our shell castle," said another.

"Don't worry, the goggles let you breathe underwater, too!"

It was true. Princess Maria could breathe and talk just as easily as the mermaids could. "It's lovely to meet you all," said Maria, following the mermaids excitedly.

# Princess Maria and the Magic Goggles

The mermaid castle was amazing. Maria and her new friends played
hide-and-seek and lots of other fun games all around it. "Let's go into the
garden and collect some shells," said Rose, the third mermaid.
"Okay," said Maria, happily. "What will you use them for?"
The mermaids all smiled at each other. "It's a special surprise," said Ruby.

The mermaids and Maria carried the shells to the surface of the lagoon.
Then, as they sat on rocks in the warm sunshine, the mermaids showed
Princess Maria how to make shell jewelry.
"It looks gorgeous," said Maria, when Lavender made a shell necklace.
Ruby and Rose had been quietly working on something together.
"Here's a special present for you, Maria," said Rose.

# Princess Maria and the Magic Goggles

"It's a shell friendship bracelet! Whenever you need friends to play with, we'll be here, waiting for you," said Ruby. Princess Maria gasped. "Thank you," she said to the mermaids. "It's just beautiful."
When the sun was very low in the sky, the mermaids said that it was time for them to swim home. Maria waved goodbye to them happily. Living at her new palace was going to be great fun after all.

# Princess Lily's Night Light

Princess Lily was scared of the dark. She knew it was silly, but each night when the queen read her a bedtime story and switched off her night light, Lily started to worry. In the dark, she imagined that there were monsters under her bed, inside her wardrobe and behind the curtains. She knew there was no such thing as monsters really, but she just couldn't stop imagining them.

One night, Lily was lying in the dark worrying, when suddenly, she saw a strange glow outside her window. It was coming from the flower bushes that grew next to the palace. "Oh, no," whispered Lily to herself. "I bet it's a strange, glow-in-the-dark monster!" Lily wished the light would just go away, but it didn't. Finally, she decided to be brave and tiptoed over to the window.

When Princess Lily looked outside, she couldn't believe her eyes.
A tiny, glowing fairy was hovering outside her window, looking
beautiful but very sad. Lily quickly opened her bedroom window.
"Hello," she said to the fairy. "Are you alright? You look upset."
"I'm lost!" cried the fairy, her eyes filled with tears. "I can't find
my way home!"

# Princess Lily's Night Light

The fairy told Princess Lily that her name was Sparkle and that she lived in a glade of purple flowers, next to a red bridge.
"I know where that is!" cried Lily. "I play there sometimes. If you follow the stream past those trees, you'll be home in no time."
"Oh, thank you so much, Lily!" cried Sparkle. "I promise I'll come back again, to repay you for your help!" Waving goodbye, Sparkle fluttered away over the treetops.

The next day, Princess Lily couldn't believe that she had met a real fairy. "I wonder if I fell asleep and just dreamed the whole thing," she thought. "Sparkle is just like the fairies I've read about in my storybook. Maybe I just made her up after all!"

That evening, after her bedtime story, Lily lay in the dark and wished with all her heart that Sparkle was real and that she would visit her again.

# Princess Lily's Night Light

Suddenly, Princess Lily saw a rainbow of glowing lights appear
outside, even brighter than the night before. Lily jumped out of
bed, ran over to the window and gasped in amazement at what
she saw. Sparkle was there, with lots of fairy friends, who each glowed
a different magical shade. "I told you I'd come back!" cried Sparkle,
"and I've brought my friends to be your special night lights!"

# Princess Lily's Night Light

"You never need to be scared of the dark again, Lily," said another fairy, called Dazzle. She had a lovely red dress and silvery wings. "We'll be here to light up the dark whenever you need us!"

"You were kind to me," said Sparkle, "so my friends and I are more than happy to help you, Princess Lily."

"Oh, thank you so much," said Lily. She snuggled down in bed, listening to her new night lights giggling softly outside and soon, she had fallen fast asleep.